Heroes of Isle aux Morts

Alice Walsh • Illustrations by Geoff Butler

Tundra Books

Published in Canada by Tundra Books, *McClelland & Stewart Young Readers,*
481 University Avenue, Toronto, Ontario M5G 2E9

Published in the United States by Tundra Books of Northern New York,
P.O. Box 1030, Plattsburgh, New York 12901

Library of Congress Control Number: 00-135457

Canadian Cataloguing in Publication Data

Walsh, Alice
    Heroes of Isle aux Morts

ISBN 0-88776-501-7

1. Despatch (Ship) – Juvenile fiction. 2. Hairy Man (Dog) – Juvenile fiction. 3. Harvey, Anne, fl. 1832 – Juvenile fiction.
4. Shipwrecks – Newfoundland – Isle aux Morts – Juvenile fiction. I. Butler, Geoff, 1945- . II. Title.

PS8595.A5847H47 2001   jC813'.54   C00-932283-3
PZ7.W34He 2001

We acknowledge the support of the Canada Council for the Arts and the Ontario Arts Council for our publishing
program.

We acknowledge the financial support of the Government of Canada through the Book Publishing Industry Development
Program for our publishing activities.

Design: Ingrid Paulson

Printed in Hong Kong, China

1 2 3 4 5 6   06 05 04 03 02 01

The Newfoundland Dog

The Newfoundland dog takes its name from the province of Newfoundland, where its breed first became known to British settlers. The Algonquin Indians were the original masters of the Newfoundlands, and a carving of the dog is at the top of one of their totems. In Algonquin legends, the Newfoundland is referred to as "the gift of the gods."

In early days, the Newfoundland was used to foretell the proximity of land. Few ships would leave port without a Newfoundland dog onboard. During World War II, the dogs were trained to lay telephone lines and were relied upon to transport ammunition.

Many famous people in history have owned Newfoundlands, including Queen Victoria, Sir Walter Scott, Charles Dickens, Edward VII, Benjamin Franklin, and Lord Byron. In fact, Napoleon was once saved from drowning by a Newfoundland.

This story, *Heroes of Isle aux Morts,* is just one account of how the Newfoundland has been celebrated as a hero; many people owe their lives to the dog's bravery. Today the Newfoundland dog has its own training academy called Black Paws Search and Rescue.

Anne Harvey was a Newfoundland girl, born to the sea. For as long as she could remember, she had fished with her father along the rugged shores of Isle aux Morts.

She loved the great sea, but she feared it too. There were dangerous reefs and shoals, and no lighthouses to guide the tiny fishing boats. Many fishermen went to sea, never to return.

Ships of every description passed by the island's massive cliffs. Sometimes Anne found silk handkerchiefs, fine linen, and pieces of china that had been washed up with the tide. They came from ships that had never reached their destination – ships that had sunk or had run aground.

Early one morning in July 1832, Anne awoke to a raging storm. Wind rattled the stovepipes and shook the glass in the windows. The great sea rose and fell. Waves rushed up to shore and thundered against the cliffs. The little fishing boats, tied to their moorings, tossed and rolled wildly.

We won't be going fishing this morning, Anne told herself. Suddenly she heard a distress signal. Then another, and another. A flare lit up the dark sky, and she knew a ship was in trouble.

Quickly she dressed and ran to the lookout at the top of the hill.

In the gray morning light, she could barely make out the ghostly shape of a ship that had been driven upon a rock. Waves smashed against the ship's side. Anne knew that if help did not arrive soon, the ship would be smashed to pieces by the savage waves.

Anne wasted no time running back to the house. Her father was still asleep, but she shook him awake. "Papa, get up," she said. "A ship has run aground."

George Harvey bolted up. "Another one?"

He had seen many shipwrecks and knew of many lives lost. In fact, that was how the island got its name. Isle aux Morts means Island of the Dead.

"Go wake Thomas," he said.

While Anne went to wake her young brother, her father put on oilskins and rubber boots. He gathered rope, a gaff, and a knife. In no time, they were all on the beach, ready to launch the dory. Hairy Man, their dog, followed them to the wharf and, when they got into the boat, he jumped in with them.

Anne took one oar and her father took the other. Together they struggled against the fierce gale. Waves broke under the boat, nearly capsizing it. At times they curled over the bow, sending showers of sea spray down upon them. While Anne and her father rowed, Thomas bailed out the water with a tin can.

As they neared the ship, they could see the word *Despatch* on her bow. They could hear the moans and cries of the frightened passengers who crowded the forecastle – the only part of the ship that was out of reach of the pounding waves. The fierce wind and rough sea kept the dory from getting close enough to help.

"We must find a way to get a rope to them," George Harvey said, anxiously. Mountainous waves crashed on the *Despatch's* deck. She was starting to go to pieces. Her lifeboats were smashed. Broken paddles and bits of wood floated around in the water.

"We could send Hairy Man," Anne suggested. "You knows what a good swimmer *he* is."

Her father nodded slowly, remembering the times Hairy Man braved the rough waters to fetch ducks, geese, and other seabirds he had shot. But from the frown that deepened her father's brow, Anne knew he held little hope for the passengers of the *Despatch*.

"Go, Hairy Man! Go, b'y." Anne pointed him in the direction of the ship.

Obediently, the dog jumped into the water and was immediately swallowed by a giant wave. Anne waited anxiously until his head rose above the churning sea. As he swam toward the doomed ship, enormous waves buried him again and again. Each time, Anne held her breath until he resurfaced.

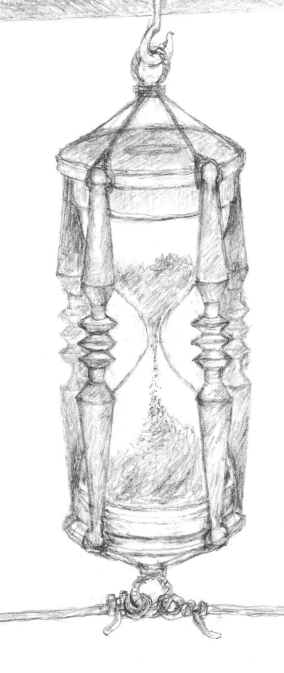

Among the passengers who huddled in the forecastle were gentlemen and grand ladies, their ruffled shirts and silk dresses ruined from the salt sea. There were men in britches and children in rags, all of them watching fearfully as the dog struggled against the violent sea.

Hairy Man did not stop swimming until he reached the *Despatch*. As eager hands lifted him aboard, a cheer went up from the crowd. A rope was tied around his middle and he was instructed to go back to his master's boat. As the dog again faced the dangerous waves, the line was carefully let out behind him.

Anne and her father rowed to shore with the rope Hairy Man had brought them. George Harvey fastened it to a pole in the ground, enabling the crew to make a breeches buoy.

Grasping the rope, one hundred and sixty-three passengers made their way, one by one, over the dangerous sea to the shores of Isle aux Morts.

The *Despatch* had come from England, on her way to Quebec. English, Newfoundland, and French voices now filled the air. Hairy Man, the center of attention, ran and hid behind the stove.

The unexpected guests stayed on the island for over a week, and all the families on Isle aux Morts shared their flour, fish, molasses, and tea. At night, in houses all over the island, the guests slept in featherbeds, on daybeds, and even on floors.

One day the supply ship came, and took the visitors away.

"Thank you for having us on your island," a gentleman said, rather formally.

"Good of yous to drop by," said George Harvey, winking at Anne.

"Good-bye."

"*Au revoir.*"

"Cheerio."

And then they were gone.

But the Harveys were not forgotten. Everywhere the passengers went, they told of their rescue by a courageous Newfoundland family and their dog. In St. John's, in Canada, and even in England, people heard of the Harveys' brave deed. Eventually, the news reached the king of England. He was so impressed by the tale that he sent them one hundred gold sovereigns. He even had a special gold medal struck for presentation, with an inscription telling of the family's bravery.

There was a personal letter for each of them, praising them for their deeds. The letter was signed by good King George: "To the heroes of Isle aux Morts."